AF378226
9 22000001 47 989

Email: uneekfortz@hotmail.com
TgosketchPress
Chicago, Illinois
www.tgosketch.com

inspired by S.L.K.T and many thanks to NW

LEMONADE

I SQUEEZE lemons TO MAKE LEMONADE.

I PRESS ORANGES NOW
JUICE IS MADE.

Flour
Sugar

I BAKE **APPLES** TO MAKE

APPLE PIE.

I POACH **PEARS** WITH THE TEMPERATURE HIGH.

Crunchy O's

I SLICE *banana* IN MY CEREAL BOWL.

I EAT **Mango** ALL ON ITS OWN.

I BLEND **strawberries** TO MAKE MILKSHAKES.

I GRATE COCONUT ON TOP OF THE CAKE.

I CRUSH *Berries* TO MAKE JAM.

I EAT FRESH **PINEAPPLES** NOT OUT OF THE CAN.

I CHOP **TOMATOES** TO MAKE SOUP.

I MAKE A FACE JUST USING FRUIT.

I PLANT **Seeds** TO MAKE FRUITS GROW.

WHAT FRUITS DO YOU LIKE?
I WANT TO KNOW.

About the Author:

Emmanuel Smart is a heating engineer. He is also a musician and used his natural talent in songwriting to create this poetic book. Emmanuel wants to motivate others to step out of their comfort zone and tap into their creativity. Too Fruity uses rhyme to teach children the many interesting ways fruits can be prepared and consumed. Emmanuel was inspired by his children to write this book as they love fruits. He hopes Too Fruity will encourage children to participate in more cooking activities and incorporate healthy choices into their lifestyle.

email: uneekfortz@hotmail.com
Too Fruity

The illustrator

Tyrus Goshay is a digital illustrator and 3d artist with over 16 years of experience. He serves as a college professor, teaching both game design, and illustration in his off time. Tyrus has his bachelors in computer animation and Multimedia, and his masters degree in teaching with technology (malt). He has contributed to several award-winning projects in the world of toy design and has been recognized for his achievements in academia as well. He also has tutorials in illustration and Digital sculpting available for training on the web.
Visit his book store and see other books that he has illustrated.

www.tgosketch.bigcartel.com

Facebook.Com/tgosketch

tgosketch@gmail.com

Instagram/tgosketch

Printed in Great Britain
by Amazon

10824789R00020